# WHERE ARE SANTA'S PANTS?

## RICHARD MERRITT

# IT'S THE COUNTDOWN TO CHRISTMAS!

Have you decorated the tree? Wrapped the presents and sent the cards? Good – because now you have to find Santa's pants!

Yes, that's right! Santa has been dieting. He is so trim and fit that his baggy, old pants keep falling off. And now he needs your help to find them.

Christmas can't go ahead if Santa's got no pants, so drop the baubles, forget the carols and join the worldwide search. There is a different pair of pants on every spread.

And that's not all! Santa's reindeer are so embarrassed, they have started behaving strangely. They are flying hot air balloons, skating on ice and generally misbehaving.

Find all eight reindeer on every page, round them up and send them back to the North Pole in time for Christmas!

And don't forget to look for the lucky sixpence. There's one on every page. But be aware, some coins are better hidden than others!

# IN THE NORTH POLE

The elves are trying to keep their minds on the job, the reindeer have run away and Santa thinks he can find his pants with a telescope. Can you spot Santa's red-and-white striped pants?

Keep an eye out for the reindeer, and see if you can spot the hidden sixpence. It might bring you luck!

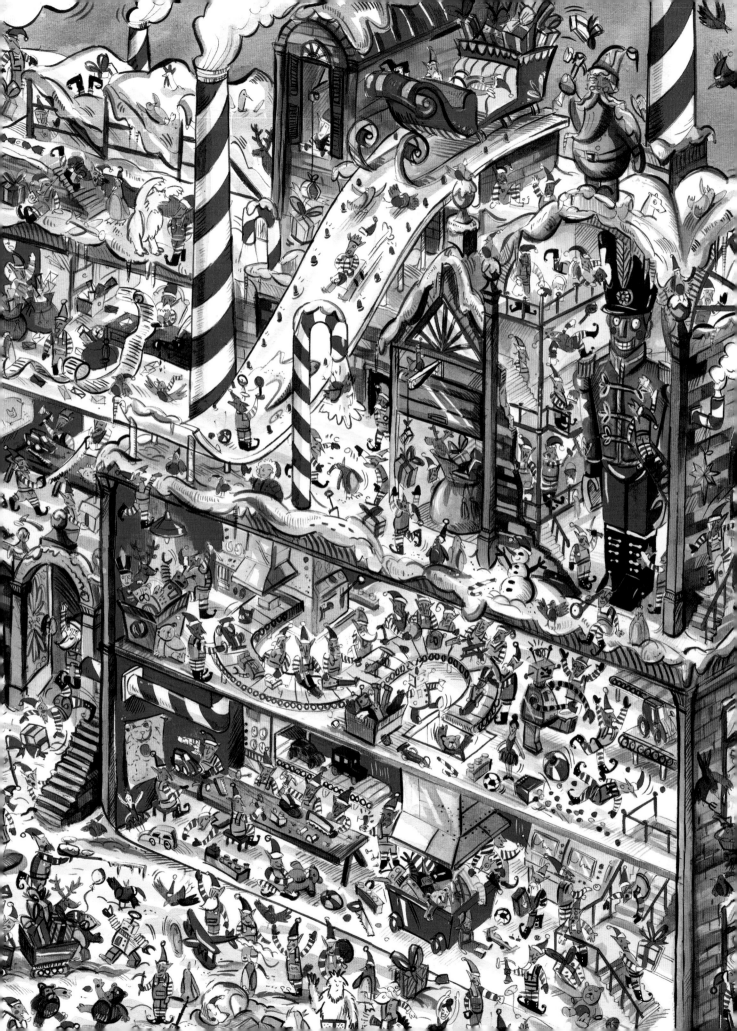

# AT THE BEACH

Before Santa has a surf, he must find his blue-and-yellow striped pants. Help him get his hands on them before they're swallowed by a shark or buried in the sand.

Find the lucky sixpence before someone takes it home for their pudding. And keep an eye out for the eight reindeer.

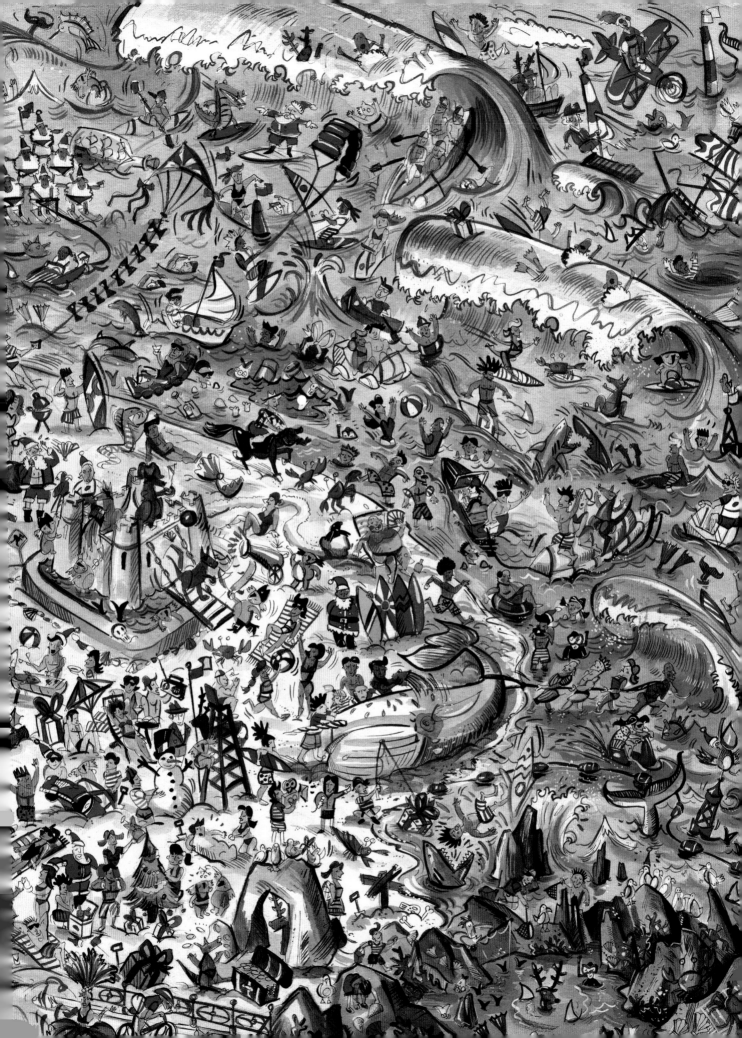

# IN THE VILLAGE

The villagers are frantically preparing for Christmas, and Santa has turned up without his pants. Can you find his blue-and-white striped pants amid the chaos?

Maybe the sixpence will help … if you can find it. And the eight reindeer are somewhere there, too!

# AT THE DEPARTMENT STORE

Hundreds of children are queuing to meet Santa, but he can't meet anyone without his red-and-white polka dot pants! Help him find his pants before they are trampled by the crowds.

The sixpence is somewhere in the building – and so are the eight reindeer.

# AT THE NATIVITY PLAY

It is tempting to sit down and enjoy the show, but there are more pressing matters at hand. You need to find Santa's purple-and-yellow polka dot pants! Don't be distracted by the mermaid … or the alien … or the robot … or the queen!

And don't forget the sixpence and the eight naughty reindeer that are hiding somewhere in the theatre!

# AT THE POST OFFICE

There are millions of parcels to be sent before Christmas, and the staff are already worn out. Santa must find his red-and-yellow striped pants before they are packaged up and sent abroad … or worse, eaten by the runaway octopus!

Find the sixpence before someone slips it into a card for their granny! And see if you can spot the eight reindeer, too!

# IN THE CITY

The city folk are going about their business, and there is so much going on that Santa can't spot his purple-and-white striped pants. Can you find them for him?

There is a sixpence somewhere in the city streets, and the eight reindeer are in some strange places!

# ON THE FARM

Farm life has never been so muddled. The pigs are sunbathing on the roof and the horse just sat down to dinner. Santa's yellow-and-green polka dot pants are somewhere in the middle of this pandemonium, and you need to find them!

Don't forget to look for the sixpence and those eight crazy reindeer!

# AT THE ICE RINK

People are having all sorts of fun at the ice rink – they're even climbing glaciers! But Santa is looking for his white-and-blue polka dot pants, and he needs you to help him find them.

Find the sixpence before it falls through a crack in the ice, and keep a lookout for the eight stray reindeer.

# AT THE TRAIN STATION

So many people with places to go and people to see! But all Santa wants are his red-and-blue polka dot pants. Find them quickly, in case someone wants an extra pair for their train journey!

If you find the sixpence, you can use it for your train fare – but don't let those eight reindeer get you in trouble!

# IN THE PARK

A visit to the park has never been so exciting, but there can be no fun for Santa until you find his green-and-red polka dot pants.

You have to find the sixpence, too – and the eight very cheeky reindeer!

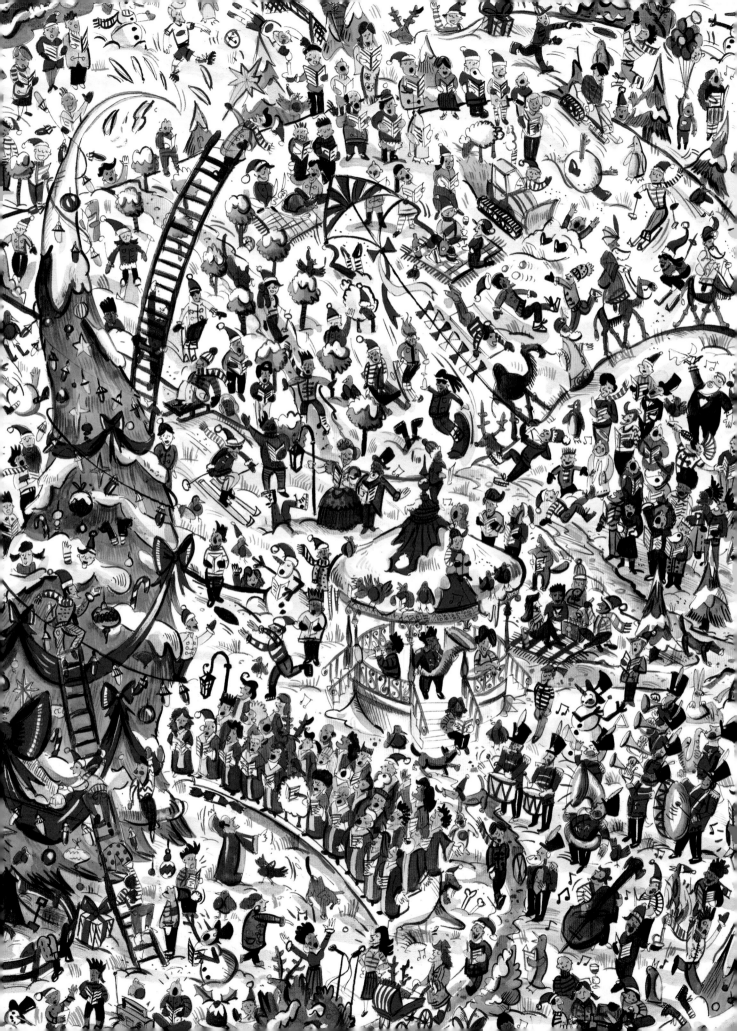

# AT HOME

No one knows when Santa lost his green-and-white striped pants. It could have been when he bobsledded off the roof, or when he went for a ride in the limousine. Can you find this last pair of pants for him?

I wonder if you are lucky enough to find the sixpence in this crazy neighbourhood. And round up those eight reindeer once and for all!

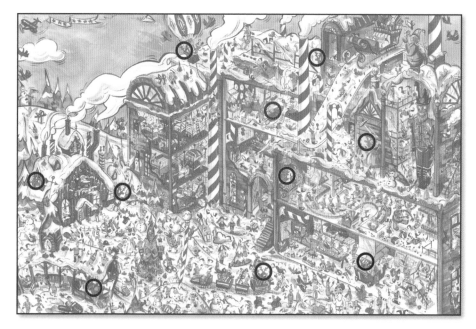

**IN THE NORTH POLE**

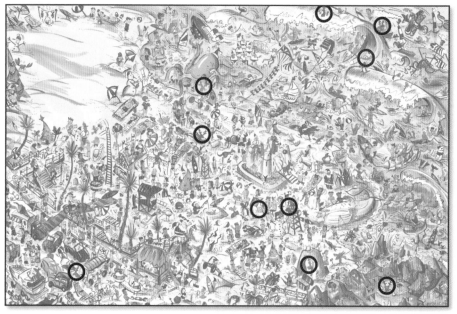

**AT THE BEACH**

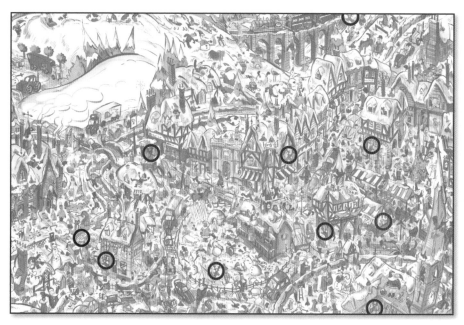

**IN THE VILLAGE**

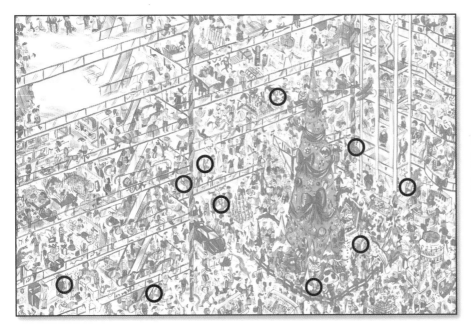

**AT THE DEPARTMENT STORE**

**AT THE NATIVITY PLAY**

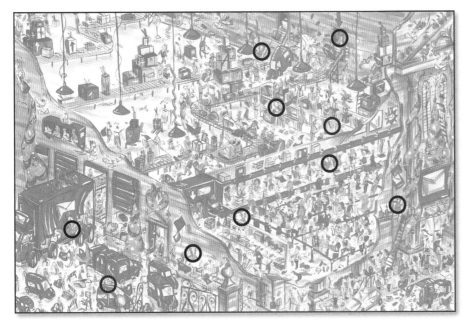

**AT THE POST OFFICE**

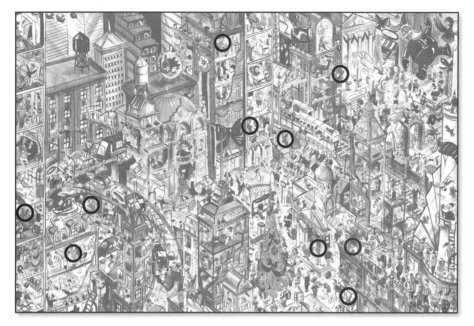

**IN THE
CITY**

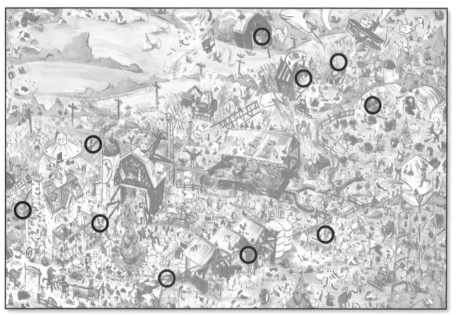

**ON THE
FARM**

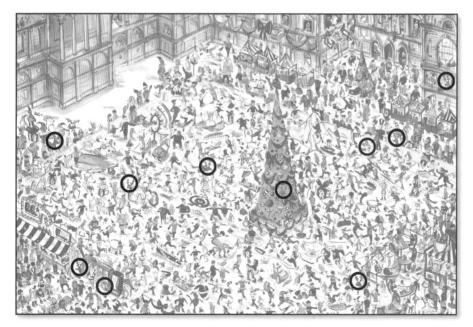

**AT THE ICE
RINK**

**AT THE TRAIN STATION**

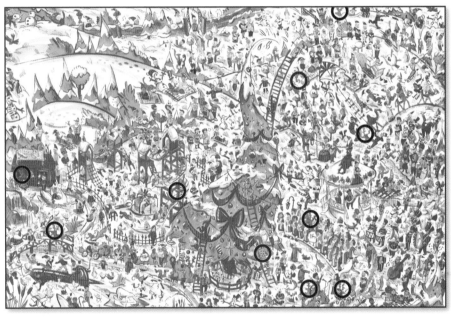

**IN THE PARK**

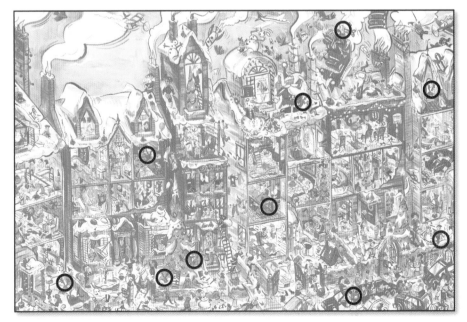

**AT HOME**

*For Nan and Gran, on your 90ᵗʰ birthdays!*

Little Hare Books
an imprint of
Hardie Grant Egmont
85 High Street
Prahran, Victoria 3181, Australia

www.littleharebooks.com

Illustrations copyright © Richard Merritt 2010

First published 2010

National Library of Australia
Cataloguing-in-Publication entry

Merritt, Richard, 1982-
Where are Santa's pants? / Richard Merritt.
9781921541506 (pbk.)
For primary school age.
Santa Claus – Juvenile fiction.
823.92

Designed by Lore Foye
Produced by Pica Digital, Singapore
Printed through Phoenix Offset
Printed in Shen Zhen, Guangdong Province, China, July 2010

5 4 3 2 1